one bear with bees in his hair

one bear with

For Vimbai and Binisa

Published by The Trumpet Club
666 Fifth Avenue, New York, New York 10103

Copyright © 1990 by Jakki Wood

For information address: Dutton Children's Books, a
division of Penguin Books USA Inc.,
New York, New York.

ISBN: 0-440-84527-0

This edition published by arrangement with
Dutton Children's Books, a division of
Penguin Books USA Inc.
Printed in the United States of America
October 1991

10 9 8 7 6 5 4 3 2 1
UPC

bees in his hair

jakki wood

A TRUMPET CLUB SPECIAL EDITION

One bear with bees in his hair.

Wait a minute—who goes there?

Two bears—that's more fun.

Oh, look! Another one.

Three hungry bears. But see . . .

Their bowls are empty. How can that be?

One bear more—that makes four.

Listen! Someone's at the door.

Open the door and see the sun.

All together, out bears run.

Five bears out of the house.

There's another, as still as a mouse.

Six bears, waltzing along,

meet a big bear whistling a song.

Seven bears having a fling.

Here comes another. She likes to sing.

Eight bears having lots of fun.

Come and join us, little one!

Nine bears playing hide-and-seek.

Close your eyes and don't you peek!

Ten bears now! For there's another,

near the tree with little brother.

That was fun—let's play again.

Close your eyes and count to ten.

Bears are hiding, near and far.

Can you see where all ten are?

One bear with bees in his hair.

Help him find the others . . . where?